COMIC TALE EASY READER:

ISBN O-943864-38-0
ISSN 0748-2264

THE HUMANIZATION OF FREDDIE MOUSE
by
Richard Blake

Illustrated by Marguerite Atcheson

Juv.
813
B58h
c. 2

SHAUGHNESSY by Nathan Zimelman

May Davenport, Editor

MAY DAVENPORT, PUBLISHERS
Los Altos Hills, California, U.S.A.

135659

© **MAY DAVENPORT, PUBLISHERS 1984**
All rights reserved. For information address;
May Davenport, Publishers, Los Altos Hills, CA. 94022,
USA

LC 81-71551
ISBN 0-943864-38-0
ISSN 0748-2264

Printed in Indonesia

ABOUT THE AUTHOR:

Richard Blake has been a journalist for many years and enjoys writing humor. He lives in San Luis Obispo, California.

ABOUT THE AUTHOR:

Nathan Zimelman has been writing children's stories for more than twenty years. Among his many published books is "If I Were Strong Enough", Abingdon Press. Mr. Zimelman lives in Sacramento, California, U.S.A.

ABOUT THE ILLUSTRATOR:

Marguerite Atcheson studied at the Chicago Art Institute, The Montgomery School of Art in Chicago, and is a free lance illustrator of children's and young adult books. She lives in South Laguna, California, U.S.A.

THE HUMANIZATION
OF
FREDDIE MOUSE

by
Richard Blake
Illustrated by Marguerite Atcheson

CHAPTER 1

If a star fell for every mouse born, 4th of July would come more than once a year. The encyclopedia discloses the astounding fact that a mamma mouse has been known to have eighteen babies all at one time! What courage! What stamina! What glorious labor pains!

The factor of 'hand-me-down' clothes is never a problem. Life's existence centers on one set of clothes — ones birthday suit.

Among the drab blacks, browns, and whites, Freddie stands out. Although his coat is black, his paws are white. Not only that, so is the tip of his tail. Anyone seeing that bit of white waving in the breeze could be assured of 'Freddie to the rescue'.

With the trend towards large families, birthday celebrations are really something. Every burning candle stood for one birthday recipient. Every child who had a birthday was responsible for blowing out his candle. Guess what was a mouse's favorite birthday cake? **Cheeseburger!** Candles on a cheeseburger? Each to his own taste.

Freddie never forgot the exciting first birthday, which included an uninvited guest. No invitations are turned down at a mouse's birthday party, not with cheeseburger as the birthday cake. A barn loft was the setting for the party.

Children were reminded, "Now mind your manners, and don't ask for second helpings." Mothers are like that.

Games were instigated to satisfy all mice. A maze of passageways was set up to see who could come up with the correct way through, in the shortest time. Of course the smartest mouse always won.

A cheese ball hunt was a favorite game, with little balls of cheese hidden in the hay. Of course, the keenest noses always won. But. the game that provided the most hilarious fun, was pinning the tail on the cat, while blindfolded. A large picture of a cat was tacked on the hayloft wall. Each in turn. attempted to pin a paper tail on the right spot Freddie had everyone squealing with laughter when he ended up pinning the tail on the cat's nose.

The climax to the party's events was when Mamma Mouse wheeled in the huge cheeseburger, with its overload of burning candles What a sight to behold! The environment was shattered by the sounds of squeaks and squeals. Children surrounded the birthday cake, ready to dive in, when the word was given. But then, something happened. The heat from the burning candles started melting the cheese. Soon, a river of the yellow stuff was running down the sides, onto the loft floor, and reaching out to envelope little mice feet. Talk about being stuck up, only here, little feet were stuck down in the gooey mess.

And, would you believe it? It had to happen now! An uninvited guest appeared on the scene — mouse's mortal enemy. A cat! She sat back to size up the situation, hissing loud enough so anyone who understood cat language got the message. "This is too good to be true. They can't get away now." Pausing to smack her lips, in anticipation of the feast before her, was a mistake. It gave the mice children time enough to lick the sticky stuff from their paws.

So, when she was ready to pounce upon the children, they were prepared. She leaped. They scampered. What happened? The cat fell flat on her face, right in the thickest of the sticky gooey melted cheese. Her mouth got filled with the stuff, leaving no option of either opening or shutting her jaws. A keen ear could have caught her frightening hiss, "Let me out of here!" Struggling loose, she made a beeline for the nearest exit.

When the signal **"all's clear"** was given, the children were permitted to return, blow out the candles, and to feast upon their hearts' desire. Little tummies got so full, it would have been hard to run away from all the cats in the world.

Everyone agreed, including Freddie, that this was the most exciting party they had ever attended.

CHAPTER 2

It is a well-known fact that all mice love cheese. But it is not a known fact that Freddie Mouse also loved cookies....dark cookies, light cookies, round cookies, square cookies, fat cookies, and thin cookies.

And just where would he find cookies? In the house where people lived, of course.

The only one who stood in his way, was Mr. Piggy-Cookie-Jar. He guarded cookies as carefully as a bank guards money. Freddie had a plan, but he didn't tell anyone about it. He didn't want to be talked out of it.

Being a smart mouse, Freddie always used the kitchen's sink drain-pipe hole for a front door. And then he used it, only in the wee small hours of the night. That was the time when people were supposed to be asleep. Snoring was sweet music to Freddie's ears, and he always listened for it before making a move. A little mouse's eyes are used to seeing in the dark, and at the hour of midnight, Freddie scampered out of the storage shed, across through the tall grass, and in no time at all was edging himself through the drain-pipe hole.

In the corner of the playroom huddled Mimi, the sweetheart of all the dolls. Mimi had a sweet gentle manner, a coy smile, and laughing eyes. Freddie never worried about waking her. She never needed any sleep, as her eyes were always open.

Freddie ran up to her, "Mimi, may I borrow your ballerina skirt for awhile?"

"What on earth would you do with a ballerina skirt?"

"I can't tell you, Mimi. It's a secret. I just want to try something. I'll take good care of it. I promise."

"Well, I guess it will be all right. But, mind you, take good care of it, and don't get it dirty."

"I promise."

Behind the closet door, Freddie wiggled into the ballerina skirt. After fastening the last button, he stepped out a little unsteadily, standing on his two hind feet. Mimi just had to giggle. After all, whoever heard of a mouse prancing around in a ballerina skirt?

With Mimi as an audience, Freddie practiced pivoting around and around on his two hind feet. It wasn't long before he was able to keep his balance. Mimi clapped and clapped. But, not one word to

Mimi of what he planned to do.

Finally, he stopped, waved goodbye, and edged his way out onto the kitchen floor. Here, he started dancing, around and around, in waltz time, counting, "**One two three, one two three.**"

High on the cupboard shelf sat **Mr. Piggy-Cookie-Jar,** in his bright yellow suit. He was round and fat. He looked like he could pop a button at any time. He was a favorite member of the chinaware set, because he always wore a jolly smile. Nobody in his right mind would ever want to hurt Mr. Piggy-Cookie-Jar... especially Freddie. But, Freddie was letting his greed get the best of him.

Mr. Piggy-Cookie-Jar looked down, and what he saw so shook him, every cookie within quivered. "Well, I'll be a Cookie's Dutch Uncle. Just what do you think you're doing?"

"Taking up dancing."

"Don't you think you look rather silly in that outfit?"

"Maybe so. But, I'm trying to make an impression."

"On whom?"

"On you."

"Oh, no!"

"OK then, sorry I bothered you." With that, Freddie slipped just a wee bit out of sight, flipping the ballerina skirt high above his skinny little legs, and spinning about on one foot.

Now, Mr. Piggy-Cookie-Jar was just as curious as anyone, and he wasn't about to miss a thing. He shifted closer to the edge of the shelf, to get a better view. As he moved closer to the edge, Freddie slipped farther out of sight.

It was bound to happen, just as Freddie hoped it would. Mr. Piggy-Cookie-Jar got too close to the edge of the shelf, and suddenly lost his balance. Down he came with a crash. His hat fell off, and cookies rolled out in all directions. The biggest cookie of all rolled right up to Freddie, and plopped right down in front of him.

"It worked! It worked!" squealed Freddie, as he reached for the cookie. But, just as he reached for the cookie, he heard Mr. Piggy-Cookie-Jar crying.

"Woe onto me. I lost all my cookies. And, I have a chip in my shoulder. I'll never be the same again."

Then Freddie realized what he had done. The plan had worked all right. But, Freddie never intended to hurt Mr. Piggy-Cookie-Jar. For the first time in his life, Freddie didn't feel very smart. He had let his greediness get the best of him. Hearing Mr. Piggy-Cookie-Jar cry made him ashamed. Gone went his taste for the cookie. With tail and ears drooping, Freddie slipped quietly over besides Mr. Piggy-Cookie-Jar. "It was all my fault. I'm sorry."

"No, it's as much my fault as yours. If I had minded my own business this would not have happened."

"Is there anything I can do to make things right again?"

Mr. Piggy-Cookie-Jar grunted sadly, "Oh,

if only you could glue me back together again."

"I'll do what I can." With that, Freddie scurried about and in no time at all had found the glue. Soon he had Mr. Piggy-Cookie-Jar looking as good as new. Well, almost.

Then Freddie picked up every cookie, pushing them down inside of Mr. Piggy-Cookie-Jar. Not once did he so much as take one little nibble. But, there was one thing he couldn't do. He couldn't put Mr. Piggy-Cookie-Jar's hat back on his head. It was too heavy. Freddie had to leave Mr. Piggy-Cookie-Jar sitting in the middle of the kitchen floor, with his hat sitting beside him.

When people got up the next morning, they found Mr. Piggy-Cookie-Jar right where he had fallen. One person turned to another, "How in the world did he fall off the shelf and still keep all his cookies?"

Only Mr. Piggy-Cookie-Jar and Freddie knew the answer, and they weren't talking!

CHAPTER 3

All children go to school, if they want to get ahead in the world, and Freddie was no exception. In fact, survival is the name of the game, when one of the required courses of study is "**How to get around a mousetrap**".

Mice are no different than people when it comes to gambling. People can lose the shirt off their backs playing around with a slot machine. Mice can lose their lives playing around with a mousetrap. Of course people are out for money.....mice, for cheese. Some tattle-tale had passed the word along that cheese was at the top of the list among mice food delectables. In the people's world, anyone who was anyone at all, kept cheese on hand, both for food and bait.

People think they're smart. They carefully avoid setting traps where household pets will step on them....where romping children will step on them.....where absentminded adults will step on them. So, always in a place where it will catch a mouse with nose trouble.

To outwit people is the name of the game, so little mice take schooling seriously. There's nothing that turn people off more, than to find an empty sprung trap. And people go stark raving mad when they come to a set trap with the cheese gone! To think that a little mouse could outsmart one is insufferable. Now that takes skill. Any mouse who can pull that gets high marks in school.

Freddie really does his homework on the subject "**How to get around a mousetrap**". His best friend, Snazzy, lost his tail in one. And Snazzy has become anti-social. After all, whoever heard of a mouse appearing in polite society minus a tail?

It should be noted that on the classroom wall hung a big picture of a mousetrap. This way, no one would ever forget what one looks like.

One day, quite by accident, Freddie discovered a solution. He arrived at school with his whiskers twitching excitedly. "Teacher-Teacher, I've got something for **'show-and-tell!'** "

"Hold it, Freddie. Don't let your whiskers get tied in knots. Let us first stand and sing, 'America'."

Everyone stood, including Freddie, and squeaked forth with:

"My Country 'Tis of Thee
Sweet land for mice to be
Of Thee I sing."

"And now, children, we'll let Freddie be

the first for **'show-and-tell'**.

Freddie beamed, "I know another way to spring a mouse-trap."

Everyone squeaked in unison, "You do?"

"That's right."

Teacher tapped her pencil. "All right children, simmer down and give Freddie a chance to share his new found discovery."

"I can give it to you in two words."

"Yes, Freddie?"

"Play ball!"

"Now listen, Freddie. This is too serious a matter to joke about."

"I'm not joking, teacher. It's as simple as that. Play ball."

"Well, I guess you need to explain yourself."

"Oh yes, teacher. Last night, the people's children were playing ball. Guess what? The ball rolled right up to a mouse-trap. And, do you know what? It sprung the trap. So, all we need to do is play ball, and let it roll in the right direction."

"You are forgetting one thing, Freddie."

"What's that?"

"Do you know any mouse who owns a ball?"

"Well, no. But, we could borrow one....after hours, that is."

"Maybe so, but what about lifting it?"

"Wouldn't have to lift it. Just give it a shove in the right direction."

"Well, you may have something there. But, let's be practical. What are the chances of finding a ball laying out on the floor after hours? It seems that in most homes, people's children are trained to put such things away at night."

"Guess I never thought of that."

"Now. that we're on the subject, this leads right into the next chapter of '**How to get around a mouse-trap.**' Take your paw and follow along. It says, 'Anything that you can lift, and drop on a trap, out of arm's reach, will do the trick.' Try it, when you get home tonight."

Guess what? Freddie didn't have to go to bed without his supper. Oh, what delicious cheese!

There are times when seeing and smelling don't always jibe, and Freddie learned that fact the hard way. The people's children had a mechanical toy. When wound up, it would play the tune 'The Farmer In The Dell'. All characters in the song rotated on a circular track, coming out of a door just when their name was sung. The mechanical toy ran down just when the hunk of cheese made an appearance. Abandoned and forgotten, the toy sat out on the playroom floor that night.

Anyone with 20-20 vision could very well spot that hunk of cheese. And, there was nothing wrong with Freddie's eyesight. In fact, he could even see in the dark.

Freddie's first reaction was, **"What sort of trap is this?"** He approached it cautiously, circling the toy several times. It was cheese all right, no question about it. But, there was one thing wrong. It didn't have any smell. Now, if there was anything better than Freddie's eyesight, it was his smeller. Freddie had had a cold, and it was just possible that his nose was stuffed up. At least that was one way to look at it.

After some time of maneuvering around, Freddie decided, "enough of this nonsense." Opening his mouth wide, he clamped down on the cheese, only to bite into a hunk of tin. "Ouch! My molars! What have I done?"

Yes, Freddie cracked his wisdom tooth. But the dentist assured Freddie's mamma, that, although Freddie had lost a wisdom tooth, he would end up being a smarter mouse.

CHAPTER 4

Although Freddie had moments of being down right stupid, he was really very smart, And, though he at times unintentionally would hurt a friend, he had a heart of gold. If he could do anyone a favor, it was always, **'Freddie to the rescue'**.

The day he met up with a baby elephant was a new experience. Neither had ever seen the likes of each other before. When Freddie walked into his presence, the baby elephant was very low in spirits.

Everybody knows, that when one is low in spirits he is down in the mouth. But, elephants are down in the trunk. On this day, Baby Elephant was stretched out on the ground, with his trunk laying flat out in front of him.

"Hi, big boy, why all the gloom?"

Baby Elephant opened one eye and gave Freddie the once over. "Where did you come from, and who are you?"

"I'm Freddie Mouse. But, you? I've never seen anyone as big as you. You must be really somebody."

"It's not what you think. Everybody laughs at me. And, do you know what I am called?"

"What?"

"Little Squirt."

"How come?"

"Well, it's a long story. You see, all elephants can squirt water through their noses. In fact, at every Fourth-of-July they hold a contest to see who can squirt water the farthest."

"So?"

"I can't squirt water. All I can do is dribble."

"So what?"

"You don't understand. Any elephant who is any elephant at all can squirt water through his nose."

"Isn't there anything that can be done?"

"I don't know. My parents thought maybe my face skin was too thin, and that possibly the sun was getting through and drying up the water."

"Well?"

"So, they decided I should wear a hat to keep the sun off of my face."

"Did it work?"

"Don't know. I can't keep the hat on my head. It keeps sliding off, whenever I move around."

"There must be some way. Let me see the hat." Baby Elephant's trunk circled around, picked up the hat, and then sat it down in front of Freddie.

Freddie ran around the hat, then crawled inside. When he climbed out he had an idea. "Know what? Maybe I can help you out. The inside of the hat has a hatband. Now, If you'll let me ride on your head, my forepaws can hang onto the hatband; my backpaws on to you. Want to give it a try?"

"I'll try anything." And do you know what? It worked. Baby Elephant pranced around, and not once did the hat slide off.

When Baby Elephant's parents saw him prancing around, they started asking questions. "How did you ever figure out how to keep the hat on?"

Baby Elephant grinned from ear to ear. "No trouble when one has help." Then he flipped his trunk around and lifted his hat, exposing Freddie Mouse. When his parents saw Freddie, they both snorted, and ran for cover. Do you know what? Elephants are scared of mice.

When word got around that a mouse was riding on Baby Elephant's head, he suddenly became a hero. Forgotten was the fact he could only dribble. After all, **wasn't** Baby Elephant the **bravest** elephant in all the world?

When Freddie found out that elephants are scared of mice, he questioned Baby Elephant, "How come you're not?"

"Well, to tell the truth, nobody ever told me I was supposed to be."

CHAPTER 5

One thing for sure, Freddie had lots of cousins. In fact, he had so many, he didn't know the names of all of them. But, he did remember **Mathew, Mark, Luke,** and **John.** They were so named because they were church mice. How come? All because they lived in a church belfry. It just so happens this is a perfect residence for mice. Their mortal enemy, cats, are too scared to climb so high. Even people are not brave enough to climb up to set a mouse-trap.

Mathew, Mark, Luke, and John, had the place all to themselves ... well, almost. Church bells also lived in the belfry. Although they took up a lot of room, they never came to life until Sunday mornings. On that day, they made up for all the days they were as quiet as a good little mouse. In fact, they made so much noise, Mathew, Mark, Luke, and John would scamper to far away places at the time they rang. That is, until someone put them wise to the use of ear-muffs. From then on, four pairs of ear-muffs hung on a nail near by. The moment the bells would begin to move, Mathew, Mark, Luke, and John would grab up the ear-muffs and clamp them over their ears.

It just so happened that Freddie picked a Sunday to come visiting. The five of them were enjoying a cup of tea, when suddenly the bells started to move. Mathew jumped up, "Don't like to rush you off, Freddie boy. But, to retain your sanity, you better make a run for it. We do not have an extra pair of ear-muffs."

The sound of the bells caught Freddie before he could make his exit. He was so scared he lost his head, and scampered over the side of the belfry opening. The tower wall wasn't the easiest surface to grab ahold of, and he kept sliding.....down...down...down.

Happily, his downward plunge was broken by falling into a flower bed. Actually, the flower bed was the top of a lady's hat. The lady was approaching the front entrance. The impact so frightened her, she cried out, "Oh Lord, I didn't mean it. Please, Lord I didn't mean it."

The man walking beside her muttered "For heavens sake, Jennie, what are you blabbering about?"

She snatched off her hat, giving Freddie a chance to slip away unnoticed. "Something hit me. I think it was the Lord's doings."

Freddie scampered through the open doors, running straight up the center aisle.

An usher spotted Freddie, and started after him, "Oh no, young feller. You're not welcome here."

The minister, relaxing in the pulpit chair, saw the mouse coming, with the usher right on his heels. He got up, walked down to the usher, putting his hand on his arm, "Never mind, Charlie, remember the church doors are open to all God's creatures."

"But, Reverend, he'll scare people away."

"Not if you don't make something of it. Pay no attention, and he'll disappear. After all, you should be giving your attention to paying customers."

"Ok, Reverend, if that's the way you want it."

The empty choir loft was a safe place for Freddie to slip into. But, not for long. Soon, the choir members began to file in, and Freddie crouched in a corner.

On this Sunday, the special music would

be a soprano solo. As the choir loft railing hid the lower half of choir members from view of the congregation, the soloist felt free to take her shoes off. Seems she felt more comfortable this way, in reaching the high notes.

Right in the middle of her solo, while hanging on to a high 'G', Freddie went into action. Mice are allergic to high tones, and Freddie wanted out. With a squeal of agony, Freddie jumped up, running across her exposed toes. That did it! Her exquisite 'G' turned into a scream as she collapsed down into her chair. A Doctor Smith was in the congregation, and he rushed up to offer his assistance.

The minister noting the wave of excitement sweeping through the congregation, stood up, held out his hand and said, "Let us close our eyes and have a word with the Lord."

While all eyes were closed, and the soloist being taken out to the choir room, Freddie slipped down the aisle and out the front door. Mathew, Mark, Luke, and John, were there to greet him. They had started a search to find out what had happened to him. Mathew peeked in, saw the hushed congregation, with bowed heads. "My gosh, Freddie. You really have a way with people. Maybe you should come and live with us, and be a bona fide church mouse."

Freddie had an answer. **"Life existence for mice is safe as long as people's eyes are shut.** But what happens if they open them?"

Come to think of it, he had a point there!

CHAPTER 6

The argument was never resolved as to whether it was **safer to live in the city or the country.** Some distant cousins field mice relations, bragged about the advantages of country living. "Man! No people to breathe down your neck. No traffic to put a crease in one's birthday suit. Carefree outdoor living with jogging facilities unlimited."

It was just by chance that Freddie had an opportunity to find out for himself, the day he got a ride, free on the house. Seems he had gotten the chills, and in an effort to hit a warm camping grounds, he had crawled up under the hood of the people's car. The engine was still warm, from a recent run, and the close warmth lulled Freddie asleep. When he awoke, he found himself in a strange land, with strange sounds. Not the usual voices of people, but animal voices, with different languages. **Sounds of cackling, crowing, mooing, grunting** .....you name it, the area had them all.

No one has ever accused a mouse of lacking a sense of curiosity, so Freddie decided to slip out from his hiding place and explore the environment. The grass being tall, and Freddie being small, he groped about aimlessly, until he ran into another mouse. They instinctively realized they were blood relations and sniffed each other in a happy how-do-you-do. When it was discovered that Freddie was a lost city guy, the offer was made to give him the grand tour.

It was truly an awakening to discover the

various shapes, sizes, smells and voices of the farm's two and four-legged creatures. The sizes scared Freddie, but his cousin assured him that everybody lived together peacefully, each to his own, with no questions asked. Of course there were risks. Get too close to a pig and he might roll over on you... unintentionally, of course. Get under a horse, and he might step on you, apologetically so. But, one took it all in stride, living one day at a time.

Freddie was almost ready to agree that country living had its points, when something happened. The two of them were slinking through the tall grass, when a hissing sound was heard. "Man! I've heard everything. But, what is this?" Sticking his neck out to get a better look Freddie could see something slithering through the grass ... something without legs! Now I've seen everything. The thing kept moving closer and closer.

His cousin yelled at him, "Hey man! Get with it! This guy is poison! He would just as soon swallow you whole, as to linger in chewing bits at a time. Let's make tracks out of here, but fast!"

Once, out of reach, the two settled down to catch their breath. Freddie turned to his cousin, "Do you have many of those things around here?"

"Oh yes, to keep alive we have to be on the alert at all times."

"You know what, cousin? I'm going to catch that ride back to the city. I couldn't stand the stress of 'here to-day, gone tomorrow!'"

CHAPTER 7

It was intolerable to think that a household would run out of cheese. So, when the lady of the house forgot to put cheese on her shopping list Freddie knew that drastic measures would have to be taken. The next time a shopping spree was in order, Freddie crawled into the shopping bag, unnoticed, of course. The lady of the house never noticed the extra weight.

After placing the shopping bag in a grocery cart, she turned her back to check commodities on the shelf. This gave Freddie a chance to slip out and go scouting.

His nose led him to where the cheese was stacked. The hunks were too big for Freddie to lift, so, the original plan to sneak some of the cheese in the cart, was knocked in the head.

Where there's a will there's a way and Freddie wasn't about to give up so easily. **Suddenly, an idea hit him.**

Guess what? Freddie climbed to the top shelf to become a part of the advertising medium. By remaining perfectly still a person would think he was part of the scenery. Everytime someone would come down the aisle he would point down to the cheese. And, it worked!

Checkout clerks were puzzled as to the run on cheese. Finally, one clerk commented to a customer, "I've never seen anything like it. Everybody seems to be buying cheese today."

"Possibly your clever display, reminding folks to pick up some cheese, has something to do with it."

"Clever display? Now you have my

curiosity aroused. I didn't know there was a setup any different than the usual run of things."

"You mean you don't know about the mouse prop being used as a reminder?"

"No kidding? This I'll have to see, when I get a free moment."

The moment she lacked a checkout customer, the girl rushed over to see the display. "Well, I'll be switched!" She climbed a step-ladder to get a closer look, reaching out to touch Freddie. He bit her on the finger; she screamed, lost her balance, and fell on the floor in a faint.

Everybody came on the run. Someone yelled, "Call an ambulance."

The floor manager arrived quickly, "Never mind folks. Just give her air, and go about your business. Thank you."

The floor manager was heard to say to another employee, "I think Maggie needs time off. She's been putting in too many hours lately."

In the meantime, Freddie decided the best thing to do was to scram. As there was no one around the meat counter, he felt safe there. In fact, safe enough to tear open a package of sirloin nuggets, for a tasty little snack. But, the meat man saw him, grabbed a broom, and gave chase, up one aisle, down another, swinging his broom.

The floor manager yelled, "Has the place gone mad?"

The meat man yelled back, "There's a mouse loose in the place. Stand back, everybody."

It was a mad house. People were bumping into each other, knocking commodities down off the shelves. Freddie? He was racing from one end of the place to the other, looking for an exit. It took a departing shopper, stepping on the automatic door opener, to open the way for Freddie's exit.

Freddie recognized the car he had come

in, and scampered up into the open window. Once, back in home surroundings, he decided it was worth it, because he heard the lady say, "One thing for sure. This time I didn't forget the cheese!"

CHAPTER 8

By the time Freddie had reached maturity, he had fallen in love with Susie, an all-white mouse. Her silky white fur was most becoming, and Freddie fell hard. But, he was very hesitant about asking her to marry him. Why? The prospect of being a father to eighteen children all at once, didn't appeal to him.... **too much responsibility.** So, they ran around together for some time, with nothing coming of it. Finally, when Susie realized there was no future in this setup, she decided to strike out on her own. She wanted to make something of her life.

It seems that white mice are much in demand, for experimental purposes. Whenever a new medicine came on the market, people tried it out on white mice first..... just in case. That's living life dangerously. But, Susie decided to volunteer her services as a laboratory mouse at the downtown medical clinic.

When Freddie heard of what she planned to do, he squeaked in dismay, "Oh, no! You can't do that. It would be too dangerous. I won't allow it."

"And, just who are you to tell me what I can, or can not do? I've made up my mind."

Freddie realized that when a woman made up her mind, that was it. He pleaded and pleaded but it was no use. The day arrived when she made her appearance at the front door of the clinic. The doorman saw her coming and held the door open for her. "We've been looking for you, young lady."

Freddie wouldn't give up. He decided to keep an eye on developments. As he had no intentions of being placed in the position of an invited guest, he got into the clinic the hard way.

In the wee hours of the night Freddie decided it was time to check up on things. Climbing the exterior of the building was no problem. The wood shingle siding made it easy for his sharp claws to dig into. Being a new building, there were no available holes. But, there was just a chance a window had been left open. Being a three-story building, there were lots of windows. But, not one of them had been left open. By the time he reached the last window on the top floor, Freddie was plump tuckered out. He stopped on the window-ledge, looked in, and what he saw threw him for a loop. There was a skeleton hanging from a wire...a human skeleton! When a guy gets scared, surprising how much additional energy he can take on. With a flip of his tail, Freddie was up on the roof in no time at all.

Sniffing here and there, Freddie came upon an air vent, with a hole just big enough to crawl into. Once inside, it was easy going. Air vents led to rooms, and in one of those rooms he would find Susie.

A mouse knows when another mouse is around, just by the squeaks. Freddie kept on squeaking until he got an answer. As he circled here and there, the squeaking got closer. Sure enough, he finally came upon Susie jumping excitedly about inside a wire cage.

"Oh, I'm so happy to see you, Freddie."

"Is everything Ok with you, Susie?"

"Well, they're feeding me good and treating me fine, but..."

"But what?"

"I'm scared."

"Why?"

"I heard one man say to another, 'We'll give her that new drug tomorrow morning at nine.' "

"And?"

"The other man said, If she lives, we'll have it made!"

"Oh Susie, we can't allow this to happen."

"What can we do?"

"Hold tight. I'll think of something They'll have to take you out of the cage to give you the drug. I'll be here. Don't worry." With that, Freddie was gone.

Shortly before nine the next morning, Freddie was hiding behind a box, in the same room with Susie. Right at nine o'clock two men in white coats, walked in. One was carrying an injection needle. This man said, "You hold her while I stick the needle in."

The other man opened the cage and reached for Susie. "Come on, little lady, science is going to bless you for this." He held Susie tightly so she couldn't squirm loose. The man with the needle was just about to jam the needle in, when Freddie went into action. He rushed out from behind the box; reaching for the ankle of the man holding Susie, he took a bite. The man jumped, dropping Susie. She landed on the floor.

Freddie squeaked, "Quick, follow me."

Once outside the building, and running down the road, Freddie said, "I'll never let you out of sight again."

You guessed it. They were married. But, Freddie was luckier than some. Only nine babies arrived to bless this union! Freddie lived long enough to see all his children grow up and take their place in the world of mice.

SPRINGTIME MAGIC
by Patricia A. Martin

In Spring my hideout comes to life,
It's cool and dark and green.
I go there when I'm mad or sad
Or just don't want to be seen.
I talk with me, or with my best friend
Whom only I can see;
We're just as cozy and just as snug
As a person and friend can be.

We eat the berries that seem to grow
Magically from the walls,
And pick spring violets from the floor
That twists through leafy halls.
And in Spring's twilight Spring Fairies come
And sing to my friend and me.
After the concert we all settle back
For starlight cakes and moonlight tea.

ABOUT THE AUTHOR
   Patricia A. Martin writes juvenile fiction, articles, as
well as poems. She teaches in the City of Poughkeep-
sie (N.Y.) Public Schools and lives in New Paltz, New
York, U.S.A.

SHAUGHNESSY

by

Nathan Zimelman

Illustrated by Marguerite Atcheson

"Who wants Shaughnessy?"

Hector Lorenzo Shaughnessy stood between two lines of boys, not looking, just waiting.

A ball was tossed into the air.

A bat swished.

The ball fell to the ground, untouched.

"That's **Shaughnessy,** batting."

The line wiggled with laughter.

A ball was tossed into the air.

A glove waved.

The ball fell to the ground, untouched.

"That's **Shaughnessy,** fielding."

The lines wriggled with laughter.

"Come on, let's play!"

The two lines of boys exploded into two teams swishing bats, thumping gloves, together.

For a moment **Hector Lorenzo Shaughnessy** stood more alone than ever.

"Hey, **Shaughnessy,**" everyone pointed to the place where umpires go, "you be the umpire."

Hector Lorenzo Shaughnessy looked at the ball flying from hand to hand. Slowly he shook his head."

"I got to go home," he said.

A very loud boy whispered in a shout, "Who wants Shaughnessy to stay?"

"We do." The two teams looked at each other. "We never finish a game for arguing if Shaughnessy doesn't umpire."

"I'm not stopping him," softly shouted the very loud boy.

"Let's go, Shaughnessy," everybody dashed about, ready to play. They stopped.

"Where's Shaughnessy?" the very loud boy loudly asked.

There was no answer. Shaughnessy had gone.

Hector Lorenzo Shaughnessy scuffled along kicking at a rock.

"Umpires wear blue suits. Umpires wear blue suits all of the time and never get to play any of the time." Shaughnessy kicked and missed.

"I'm too young to wear blue suits, unless it is Sunday." Shaughnessy took a skip and a hop back to a stop before the rock. Carefully he drew back his right foot.

"Boom!" said Shaughnessy and kicked with all of his might. Off the side of his shoe flew the rock, fast and faster and...

"Right into Mr. Goldberg's yard," Shaughnessy sighed. "I don't kick so good either."

"It's only dirt, Shaughnessy," Mr. Goldberg waved a small wave where the rock was now resting. "Dirt you can't hurt."

"How come the flowers are missing, Mr. Goldberg?" asked Shaughnessy.

"Now there's a good reason." The watery sun of spring shone on the brown unturned ground. "Here I plant the flowers of summer."

"In the summer there will be a better reason?"

"With my aches who can bend to plant?"

"I can. See, Mr. Goldberg." Shaughnessy bent and dug at the rich brown of the earth with his fingers.

"With a trowel would be better, Shaughnessy," said Mr. Goldberg. "And with my directing and your digging, it will be better yet. Summer will positively beam," beamed Mr. Goldberg.

"Let's begin," said Shaughnessy.

"Red would look nice there," pointed Mr. Goldberg.

Shaughnessy dug a hole and patted in a bulb.

"Yellow would look nice here, Mr. Goldberg," Shaughnessy dug another hole.

"Bad it wouldn't be," nodded Mr. Goldberg. "Here's a bulb. Plant in good health."

"Red and yellow and gold and blue and won't summer be something." Shaughnessy slapped the dirt off of his hands.

"Without Shaughnessy such a summer it would have been. However," Mr. Goldberg looked ahead to the lovely summer to come, "Shaughnessy was wanted, and Shaughnessy was here."

"So where is Shaughnessy?"

Hector Lorenzo Shaughnessy had heard a sound. With his nose nearly touching the grass Shaughnessy went following the sound, looking to see what he had heard.

He saw a snail chewing a dandelion leaf, quietly.

He saw a grasshopper hopping, quietly.

The sound grew louder.

Wildflowers rushed through the grass, quietly.

Ants marched to work, quietly.

The sound grew louder.

The sound grew as loud as a baby bird fallen from its nest, flopping wildly about the grass.

Shaughnessy, who never could field the gentlest roll of a baseball scooped. And there in his hand lay a trembling of feathers.

"Straws in a tree is where the nest will be," said Shaughnessy looking as high as he could look.

There was no golden straw nest to be seen among the new green leaves.

The bird chirped in the warmth of Shaughnessy's hand.

"You've got nothing to worry about," said Shaughnessy. "Once I find your nest you'll see what a good climber I am."

"There it is," said Shaughnessy following the point of his nose to the gold of the straw in the green of the leaves.

"In you go," said Shaughnessy putting the bird down the buttoned up front of his shirt, size ten years.

Shaughnessy was eight.

Up Shaughnessy climbed, all care and elbows and knees, a clutch and a pull and a scramble until the glimpse of straw grew into a nest holding three noisy young birds.

"One," said Shaughnessy, reaching down into his shirt and pulling out a bird, "plus three makes four birds in a nest."

"Cheep, cheep, cheep," called the four birds in their nest.

Blue in the blue sky above the mother bird wheeled in a wide arc. Down she swooped. Her four children, their beaks opened wide, told of Shaughnessy. Her bright eyes pecked about, seeking. Shaughnessy was not to be seen.

"Children," she said and plopped a worm into each wide open beak.

Shaughnessy skittered out of the tree.

"I smell paint," sniffed Shaughnessy.

"Where there is fresh paint something good is happening."

Sniffingly, Shaughnessy went along until he arrived at a window of endless glass.

"Yesterday," said Shaughnessy, "it said **BAKERY**.

Flakes of paint colored the sidewalk below the window. The window didn't say anything.

"No! No! No!" said a floury man jumping up and down upon a baker's hat. "First, ever first, shall be painted the name of Mr. Claude."

"Yes! Yes! Yes!" shouted a similar man jumping up and down upon a baker's hat. "Only after the name of Mr. Henri shall be painted the name of Mr. Claude.!"

"You getting a new sign, Mr. Claude and Mr. Henri?" asked Shaughnessy.

Mr Claude snatched the paintbrush from the sign painter's fingers and curved a C upon the tip of Mr. Henri's nose.

"Shaughnessy," he said, "the Petite Patisserie, this so small bakery, will have a new sign when the sign reads Mr. Claude's and Mr. Henri's Petite Patisserie."

Mr. Henri plucked the brush from Mr. Claude's fingers. Rapidly he stroked three lines. An H appeared on the tip of Mr. Claude's nose.

"Shaughnessy," he said, "when the sign reads Mr. Henri's name and Mr. Claude's Petite

Patisseries, only then will there be a new sign."

"Everybody knows who you are," said Shaughnessy.

"But of course," Mr. Henri twirled his large mustaches. "We are Mr. Henri and Mr. Claude."

"Mr. Claude and Mr. Henri," Mr. Claude furiously tugged his small beard.

Shaughnessy pressed his nose against the signless window and looked at the wonders within licked his lips.

"You are the two greatest bakers in the whole world," said Shaughnessy.

"But of course." Mr. Henri and Mr. Claude danced about, arm in arm.

"Mr. Painter, why could you not see as Shaughnessy could see. Paint it so, **The two greatest bakers' Petite Patisserie**.

"Your hands, Shaughnessy, both left and right, to be shaken by the hands of the two greatest bakers in the world."

"Shaughnessy."

"Shaughnessy."

Mr. Claude's hand and Mr. Henri's hand closed upon air. Shaughnessy was gone.

Mrs. Amalia Schomburg, a very large lady, was proceeding down the street.

And Shaughnessy knew what was going to happen.

"There goes Charlie," said Shaughnessy as it happened.

Fat Little Charlie Schomburg tore free from his mother's firm grasp and away he sped.

"Help! Help! wailed Mrs. Amalia Schomburg jiggling after fat little Charlie Schomburg.

"Help! My darling Charlie will be run over."

"For a fat kid he sure can run," gasped Shaughnessy in pursuit. "It's a good thing I know so much about football and catching runners."

"Shaughnessy is cutting diagonally across the field," breathlessly broadcast Shaughnessy who watched television every football Sunday.

"Shaughnessy is closing the gap. Shaughnessy saves the touchdown," gasped Shaughnessy reaching out and collaring fat little Charle Schomburg.

"An angel, he's an angel sent from Heaven in answer to a mother's prayer." Mrs. Amalia Schomburg jiggling up clamped a firm hand on little Charlie Schomburg.

"Shaughnessy," she reached out a hugh hug, "what can a mother say? Shaughnessy?"

A smacking kiss always followed a hugh hug.

Shaughnessy was gone.

Shaughnessy hurried, counting houses down familiar streets.

He came to where he had to come.

He jumped two steps and climbed one.

Softly, he opened a screen door and a regular door.

"I'm home," said Shaughnessy.

"What shall I do? What shall I do?"

Splendid in her Sunday hat, which sat somewhat askew upon her head, his mother fluttered through the house flittering her hands.

"I have to go to a meeting and the baby sitter has cancelled out at the last minute.

"I have no one to watch baby. And it is an absolutely **must** meeting."

"I'm here," said Shaughnessy.

"Hector . Lorenzo Shaughnessy," his mother straightened her splendid Sunday hat upon her head and headed for the door, "you certainly are."

The regular door slammed.

The screen door slammed.

Shaughnessy's mother was gone.

Shaughnessy went into his baby sister's room.

She stood up in her play pen and held her arms out.

Shaughnessy took her in his arms.

"You know," said Shaughnessy, "it's nice to be wanted."

THE END

other COMIC TALE EASY READERS :

(Mail order to May Davenport, Publishers, 26313 Purissima Road, Los Altos Hills, CA., 94022. Add 15% postage and handling plus 6½ % sales tax if resident of California.)

The Secret Flower of Ranatan by Herbert L. McClelland; Kerri, a lonely youngster, explores a field behind her house and discovers a magic kingdom with many unusual playmates. Cartoons as visual aids may assist slow readers. Fun-to-read alone or aloud; 52 pg, orig, papbk, ISBN 0-943864-09-7, ISSN 0748-2264, $3.50

The Magga Birds of Ranatan by Herbert L. McClelland/**Why do we not see any little people, Miss Wintergreen?**" by Nathan Zimelman/**Spots and Splashes and a Million Butterflies** by Joyce Deedy; Magga Birds paralyze many in the land of Ranatan, but Kerri intervenes and solves the mystery./Librarian succeeds in luring children into her library by demonstrating what she learned from books./Monarch butterflies go south, like birds...three stories are imaginative, entertaining; 82 pg, orig papbk, ISBN 0-943864-10-0, ISSN 0748-2264, $3.50.

Rocky Duck and **Santa's Gift to the Littlest Penguin** by Evelyn Witter/**Have You Ever Fallen In Love?** by Eva Neal. Rocky, a duckling, dislikes waddling, but finds it better than skittering, strutting, leaping./Alvin, an armadillo, finds love pleasant. Rocky has simple cartoons to color; other stories, easy-to-read alone or aloud; 66 pg, orig. papbk, ISBN 0-943864-16-X, ISSN 0748-2264, $3.50.

ABC of Ecology written and illus, by Frances Wosmek; the alphabetized visuals are decorative to color; the text is individualistic and poetic. Easy-to-read; 27 pg, spiral bind, ISBN 0-943864-43-7, ISSN 0748-2264, $2.50.